Memory of a Scent

A short science fiction story

Ryan M. Williams

Glittering Throng Press

Glittering Throng Press
PO BOX 179 RAINIER WA 98576-0179

eBook ISBN-13 978-1-946440-78-5
Paperback ISBN-13 978-1-946440-79-2

MEMORY OF A SCENT

GTP NO. 43
SGC NO. 01

Contents

1

GR-ND—"Pops" to the barefoot kids that trampled the sun-cracked asphalt streets—stumbled along on feet made unsteady by erratic servos and worn bearings. Each step made a *scritch-scree* noise in his left knee. Audible to his working pickups, but lost in the clamor and noise of the street even at this early hour. Taxi flits landed hard, disgorging or picking up passengers, then bounced skyward in a buzz of strained displacement drives. Like a nest of yellow-and-black hornets that came and went from the hard-packed ground among the dried grass of his home, back when he was a meat-blood kid not that different from those darting past, squealing, laughing, outwardly sightless beneath their visors.

What did the street look like to them?

Pops didn't bother looking. He had to get home. Recharge. Make sure Mary ate something today other than protein pastes. *Real food.* He carried two red tomatoes, a small onion, and a pepper in the cloth bag clipped to his side. Enough to add some color and life to her breakfast. She'd looked so drawn lately.

"Worn and stretched out until my bones splinter," she said, in his replay. "Best get moved on soon."

"Not yet," he told her. *Not yet.*

"Better, isn't it?"

"Sure, sure," he told her. "Better than the alternative."

His knee went *scritch-scree, scritch-scree.* He stumbled again, and telescoped an arm out to catch the wall of the antiques shop he was passing. He regained his footing and retracted the arm.

Better than dead.

That'd been the promise. Not knowing what death was actually like, Pops wasn't sure whether the promise had been kept or not.

Hot air blew a dust devil along the cracked street. People of all types stepped aside or walked through. The dust devil broke apart. Pops ran quick diagnostics on his leg, knee, ankle, and foot servos and systems. Too many amber alerts. Nothing that couldn't be bypassed or ignored for another day. The dust didn't help. Got in joints and the grit scored the surfaces. Turned smooth to rough.

A big man—meat-blood-fat (over thirty percent)—towered up in front of Pops, unexpectedly interrupting the diagnostic check. Lighter-hued than many people Pops saw, splotchy dark areas on neck and hairy arms suggesting auto-immune or environmental damage. Hair made a dark halo in an arch from ear-to-ear, shaved in front and back. Visor looked almost embedded in the folds of flesh above and below the dark shades. The hairy halo continued beneath his jaw from ear-to-ear, chin and face bare. He wore a glittery blue robe of sorts, sleeveless, that hung to his knees. Tough black boots swallowed the thick calves.

"U got there?" A finger with three ring monitors pointed at the Pops' bag.

"Excuse me?"

"Watt u got there?"

Pops said nothing. He turned and took a step away from the shop, intending to go around the man.

A metal bar clanged against his chest plates. He stopped, surprised, and saw the man held the bar. A replay check showed the man had worn it on a loop at his side, partly hidden by the robe. Not that it mattered where he'd gotten it, he had it. And used it to block Pops' path.

Several people looked, visors flashing in the light, and turned away. Kids skidded to a halt. Visors fixed and recording the confrontation.

Pops stepped back from the bar. His knee went *scritch-scree* with the movement.

"I am filing a report with the authorities on your illegal assault," Pops coldly informed the man.

His assailant pressed the bar against Pops' chest and gave him a shove with it. Pops stumbled backward, knee doing a louder *scritch-scree*. "So? U ansur. Watt u got?" The bar prodded at the cloth bag.

Pops twisted away. "That isn't any of your business."

"Is food?" the man persisted. "U dead-can. Don't eat, true?"

"I don't eat, no," Pops said. "Not that it is any of your business. My wife, however, is very much alive. She does eat."

"Not today." The man lunged forward, quick despite his bulk, snatching with his free hand at the bag. Thick fingers caught the fabric and held. Pulled. Pops went with the bag. The clip welded to his frame. The bag a reinforced polymer wool blend. It wouldn't tear.

"Hey!" Pops reached down about to grab the man's wrist. He stopped, metal fingers a centimeter above the fleshy wrist, unable to close his grip. An alert flashed. *Unauthorized action. Cease immediately.*

Well, shit. Pops reached instead for the bag and grabbed it as the man yanked, throwing him off balance.

"Stop it!" he said, static from the strained servos cracking his voice. "Release me!"

Another yank nearly pulled Pops into his attacker. He locked his legs in place. The next yank failed to move him. The man raised the metal bar high above his head, about to bring it crashing down on Pops. He lifted an arm to ward off the blow.

Shrill whistles and sirens sounded above. Red and blue lights strobed against the concrete and glass buildings as police flits descended.

Growling, the man released his grip on the bag and sprang away. Not for the street, but the cover of the wall. The sudden release of tension sent Pops falling back. His legs couldn't unlock quickly enough. He dropped, landing on his rear with a loud clang. He saw his assailant slip into a dark alley between the antique shop and the massage parlour next door, turning his bulk sideways to fit in the narrow space.

"I hope he gets stuck," Pops said to no one. The onlookers had moved on, melting into the crowd as the police flits touched down on the street.

Officers—meat-blood and dead-cans both—moved quickly out of the vehicles and closed on Pops where he sat on the ground. With helmets and body armor, they didn't look that different from one another. Except the legs and arms on second look showed mechanical joints beneath the armor plates. None of them had trouble moving or made noises from sand grit and worn bearings. Pops pointed past them, at the alley.

"He went in there."

One of them spoke. "Sir, witnesses report a mentic attack on a person. Please submit to log scan."

"I didn't do anything! That man attacked me."

Officers on each side moved quickly. Metal fingers beneath the gloves seized Pops shoulders and applied force to keep him where he was sitting. "Come on, this isn't—"

A hand (flesh beneath the glove) shoved his head forward to expose the auxiliary socket. Pops' feet beat uselessly against the concrete. An icy cold needle pierced his neck and his thoughts, shattering any coherent thread into bright splinters.

2

Sparkling fragments of thought realigned themselves and melded back into a whole like a shattered glass reassembling itself into a window. Pops' first clear thought reached his awareness. *My vegetables. Where—*

His questing fingers found the tough weave of the bag. It still hung from the clip on his side. That man had tried to take it from him. He had resisted. Then the man fled when the police—

Pops' visual systems came back online to bright light from the strip of bleached sky overhead. Sunlight beat down on the old asphalt, flickering as flits came and went.

Like hornets.

TIME SYNC

Ten minutes had passed since the cop stabbed him with the log scan needle. No sign of the police. They'd already left. Scanned him and left him sitting on the pavement. A child giggled.

Pops identified the sound. It came from the little dark-haired girl that stood a meter away from him, fine features smeared with dirt, eyes a bright turquois that had to be the result of genetic modifications. Like many of the children in the neighborhood, she was barefoot, wearing the once-white overalls popular with the kids. Maybe six, seven years old. Her visor was shoved up over her forehead. When she opened her mouth he saw that she was missing some teeth.

"You doing okay, Pops?" Her voice lisped at the end. Mary always wanted a license for a girl. Never could afford it on their income.

This girl was likely unlicensed. Many of the kids roaming the street were un-licensed. Not *technically* orphans. The people in the neighborhood cared for them in a benign neglectful sort of way. The government saw to it that they had visors to access their lessons. A path into some sort of life for those with the incli-nation and sense to take advantage of it. A fun game for the rest.

His diagnostic system showed the usual amber alerts. Nothing that pre-vented him from functioning, if at a decreased level. He dismissed the report from his awareness.

"I think so, child. I fell down when the man let go."

"Pols stuck ya," she said, tapping the back of her neck to illustrate the point.

"Yes. They wanted a log scan to check my story. Thought I might have attacked that man."

She shook her head. He wasn't sure what she meant by it, not that it mattered too much. He tested his legs, found they worked as well as he could reasonably expect and climbed to his feet. The girl stepped back and peered up at him.

"Got sweets, Pops?"

That was the common refrain from kids. He saw others in the moving crowd, ducking behind taller adults making their unseeing way past him on either side, watching to see if he did have sweets. Maybe sweets in the bag that the man tried to steal. Sent her out with her turquois eyes to ask him.

"Not on me, no," he said.

Her shoulders rose and fell in an odd rolling motion that started on her right and ended on her left. "'s okay."

Mary would be waiting back home. He needed to get back to her. Seeing this child might brighten her day. She loved it when the children came to visit.

"If you want to walk with me, you may. I have sweets at home. I'll give you one when we get there."

"Sweets?" She asked the question as if not believing him.

"That's right," Pops said. "Walk me home, and you get a sweet."

She clapped her grimy little hands together. "Goodie!"

Pops started walking and his knee went *scritch-scree* with every other step. Despite the crowds, the girl had no problem matching his speed. At times she skipped ahead, becoming almost lost in the crowd. Pops grew concerned and then he would see her, standing among the taller, busy adults, waiting for him, a bright smile on her face getting bigger every time she saw him.

Other children followed like a pack of hunting wolves. They moved with more skill among the crowd. Sometimes ahead, sometimes behind, but close by as Pops and the girl covered the next few blocks to his building.

She had already stopped outside the door, waiting for him to catch up, as if she knew without a doubt which building he lived in. It wouldn't surprise him. Even in this day and age, the sight of a mentic—what he was, a living human brain in an artificial body—was rare. He'd seen the rumors about mentics that could convincingly mimic real live people here and today. He wasn't like that. No one would doubt what he was when they saw him. Too old and antiquated to pass for the genuine article they promised. Too robotic. A horror show. The dull ache persisted in his joints as he approached the door.

Carl, the building's door man, stood blocking the entrance, arms folded and face set in an expression of calm patience. Carl had the kind of build that you used to see on professional wrestlers. His tailored uniform fit him very well, ever crease immaculate. Next to him, Pops knew that he and the girl both looked like something washed up from the lake.

That didn't spoil Carl's pearly white smile that transformed his broad face into a welcoming beacon.

"Mr. GR-ND, welcome back. Who is your beautiful little friend?"

The girl moved back away from Carl and hid her face. Pops knew it was too late for that sort of thing. The building systems had tagged her the instant she was in range. Carl likely knew more about her than he did.

"A new friend," Pops said. "I told her I'd get her a sweet."

Carl said, "That's very kind. What about it, Miss? What do you call you? I'm Carl. You already know Pops."

The girl peeked, eagerness for a sweet tempting her to look up at Carl's towering bulk. "Daphne."

Daphne. That rang a bell. He'd seen her before. Months ago. Shy. Came up to him when he was passing out some sweets to the unlicensed kids. She'd grown since, lost a couple teeth.

Pops knee went *scritch-scree* as he turned and he wobbled. Carl's big hand caught his shoulder, steadying him. "You ought to get that looked at Mr. GR-ND. Doesn't sound right."

"It's not. I will." He needed to check on Mary first. He looked at Daphne. "Wait here with Carl. I'll be right back down with your sweet, okay?"

Daphne looked around up and down the walk in front of the building. Pops picked up movement among the crowd from other unlicensed children out there, trying to stay out of sight. He knew from experience that they would come out of hiding as soon as he produced the candy.

"Okay," she said.

"Wonderful," Carl said. "You can keep me company until Pops gets back."

Nodding to Carl, Pops wobbled on stiffened knees into the building, doors automatically opening and closing behind him. Sensors showed the temperature inside the building was twenty degrees cooler than outside. The grinding noises in his joints sounded louder in the relative quiet of the building's lobby. It wasn't busy this time of the day. A few people at the tables in front of the coffee shop, singly and a few groups in twos and threes. People Pops recognized from the building. None did more than glance his way as he walked to the elevators.

Only two floors up to reach their apartment, he could have taken the stairs, except for his worn-out joints. Would have years ago, freshly awakened in his new body. It'd been a miracle at the time. Able to move so easily without pained joints. He chuckled softly to himself. The elevator door chimed, slid open, empty inside. He entered.

3

DUST MOTES DANCED IN the air, light by the filtered sunlight through the living room window. It was quiet in the apartment. No sounds registered on his pickups other than the noise of his own movement.

"Mary?" His voice sounded loud in the stillness. He kept walking, left knee failing to flex fully with each step, giving him a limp, into the kitchen. He detached the bag and unsealed the catch, drawing it open to take out the vegetables.

The pepper placed on the counter was a healthy bright orange. Onion small, but white beneath the papery skin. The tomatoes bright red and smooth-skinned, though one had a bruise on one side. Casualty of the assault. Lucky, that the only real damage done. Pops felt a surge of pride that the thief had failed. The police had log scanned him—that was the worst of the whole incident. Except he was fine. Good. Daphne waited downstairs. He needed to get the candy and go back down. Power levels would suffice until he could get back up here to recharge.

"Mary?" Leaving the vegetables and the bag on the counter, Pops left the kitchen, entered the hall and started back to Mary's bedroom. "Are you hungry? Did you eat already?"

His knee went *scritch-scree*. The left unlocked, grit shifting out of the way. At the bedroom door, Pops stopped. He raised a hand to knock, but paused to listen.

He picked up the rhythmic sounds of her CPAP helping her breathe. *Still asleep.* He lowered his hand and turned from the bedroom without opening the door. He went in search of candy.

The old tin can with it's bright labeling sat in his hand, the silvery insides empty. No candy. He thought back. It'd been half-full the last time he took out candy to give to the kids, hadn't it? He remembered the golden crinkle of the plastic over the butterscotches. The sweet buttery taste flooded his memory and triggered no responses in his body. No mouth or salivary glands to water at the memory of sucking the candy. It was a clear memory of the taste. The sound of waves against a shore and salty air. Voices mingling with laughter and the cries of sea gulls.

Sea gulls. Decades ago now, he couldn't be sure how many. Long enough that there were no more sea gulls. Or birds at all. Descendants of avian dinosaurs that had survived the meteor impact, brought to an end by habitat destruction, climate change, and avian flu. The trifecta on top of other stresses from pollution, toxins, and the collapse of food supplies.

Pops put the tin can down beside the lid. No butterscotches? Did they have other candy? He had promised Daphne, and by extension the other kids. Maybe Mary had eaten the last of the butterscotches. It wasn't like her, but she'd been confused lately. Maybe she decided that she liked the candy.

He opened the cupboard above, looking for other cans. They had bought several the last time. There weren't any in the cupboard. Or much of anything at all. The protein packets were in the refrigerator. Algae-based nutrient packets ready to mix with flavor packets and solidifiers in the printer.

Pops looked at the printer attached to the refrigerator. He could print candies, except that would take too long. He couldn't leave Daphne downstairs that long. She'd think he wasn't coming back. It'd already taken longer than he had expected.

He opened the doors on the other three cupboards in the kitchen, searching for any other butterscotch containers. There must be more, somewhere. It couldn't all be gone. He found empty, dusty spaces, one after another, except for the third, which held a packet of unopened mousetraps—the old kind that was a piece of wood with a metal spring and an arm that held the spring until a mouse touched the bait. Or your fingers, half the time when setting the trap. Illegal now, of course, given the endangered status of common house mice.

Although with the food printer there wasn't much in the way of anything to attract a mouse anyway, if there were any still around.

He didn't touch the traps. Throwing them out would invite trouble if their trash was inspected. Better to leave them at the back of the cupboard in their sealed package to gather dust. Then, at least, they could argue that the traps were a relic left there by a previous occupant. You couldn't even buy those today.

It didn't help.

Pops straightened with an audible grinding noise. A warning flashed through his systems. He needed to recharge. And needed to fix a breakfast for Mary. Except Daphne and the other unlicensed children were downstairs, believing he would come back with sweets, with the candy. He could call down, tell Carl to let them know he was out of sweets. He would get some another day.

Pops stood for several seconds, head bowed, composing the message to text to Carl. Then deleted it unsent.

He had to tell Daphne himself and apologize.

After he checked on Mary. If she was awake, he would tell her that he would be right back and would fix her something special after he spent a few minutes recharging.

4

THE ELEVATOR THUDDED TO a stop. The doors chimed and slid apart to reveal the lobby. Pops carefully held the tray in his hands, watching each step. He wouldn't stumble even though his knee went *scritch-scree* every few steps. Steam rose from the tray and wafted past him. Sensors picked up the increased humidity and automatically analyzed the composition, listing the molecules present. Not the same thing as smell. Still, it triggered memories filed away in Pops' net. Molecules associated with stored scent memories evoked those recollections. It was the memory of a scent, rather than the scent itself, but that was something.

Actually, it described him too. And Mary, soon.

Red and white lights flashed outside the building. Emergency flits landing on the cracked asphalt. Pops moved to one side as emergency responders piled through the door.

"Second floor," he called, giving them the apartment number. "It's open. Mary is in the bedroom, on the left. I'll be right up in a minute."

A man stopped. Young, meat-bone, dressed in a dark blue t-shirt and pants. Muscles pressed against the fabric of his shirt. He had a pale blue-gray visor covering his eyes and short-cropped dark hair.

"You are?"

"GR-ND," Pops said. "Mary is my wife. We have an embodiment policy.

The information is all in the information cube beside the bed."

"Understood. We'll evaluate and transport her to the nearest embodiment facility if her condition can't be stabilized."

"She has a DNR to go with the policy," Pops said.

"Very well. Where are you going?"

Pops lifted the tray a few centimeters. His neck creaked when he nodded in the direction of the door. "Something for the children. I'll be back in a minute."

His charge indicator turned critical. He said, "Excuse me, I don't have much time. I need a recharge."

"Go ahead," the man said, already turning away. "We'll check on your wife."

Pops turned to the doors and his knee went *scritch-scree*. Each step he took was slow at such low power levels. He might have to ask Carl for a hand getting back upstairs.

He made it to the doors and outside. The flits had drawn a crowd of a few onlookers. Carl turned and looked down at him as he came out. He eyed the tray.

"That's not sweets," he said, rubbing his jaw.

"No. Better than sweets. Real food."

Carl's eyebrows raised. "Real?"

"Grown, not printed. The vegetables at least. Not the egg substitute."

Pops looked around at the crowd, not seeing Daphne.

Carl pointed off to the other side, close to the corner of the building. Pops turned that way. Saw Daphne's tiny elfin face peek around the corner.

"It's okay," Pops called to her. "I made something for you."

Emboldened, Daphne emerged around the corner. A pale-faced little boy with ghostly dark eyes followed her, holding her coveralls, one finger stuck in his mouth.

"Here," Pops said. "Before they get cold."

Daphne hurried her steps. The smaller boy keeping up with her and never releasing his grip. They reached the entrance and Pops bent his protesting knees and lowered the tray so they could see what he had.

"What is it?" Daphne said, eyes narrowed. She sniffed. "Not sweets."

"No," Pops said. "I'm sorry, I ran out. This is better anyway. Omelets. Try one. I think you'll like them. My Mary does, but she won't need to eat any more."

Daphne reached out, paused, and squinted up at him. He saw the gaps where she was missing teeth. "Why not?"

"She'll be like me. Embodied. So we can stay together, in a way."

"Okay." Daphne poked one of the small round omelets he'd made with the vegetables and printed egg substitute. It looked right. Mary always said she loved them.

The child picked one up and took a small nibbled bite. Her eyes widened and then she beamed at him, wide and bright despite the missing teeth.

"It's good!" She picked up another one and pushed at at the little boy. "Eat this."

The boy obeyed, with less hesitation, taking large bites. Daphne finished hers in three quick bites, eyes already going back to the remaining omelets on the tray.

His power levels warned of system shut downs.

"Take them all," he said. "Give some to your friends. I need to go recharge and see to Mary."

"Thanks!" Daphne said. She scooped up the rest of the cooling omelets and then she and the boy raced off into the slowly dispersing crowd.

Pops stumbled and found a strong hand steadying him. Carl's face looked dim. "Recharge."

Carl nodded and said something Pops couldn't make out. Then his visual feed shut down, leaving him blind as well as deaf. There wasn't time for fear. His other systems were shutting down to preserve his core net and his brain function.

5

Light returned with a rush as GR-ND's systems rebooted and came online. His core net loaded his cognitive, personality, and memory routines. He began processing and interpreting the inputs from his sensors and internal diagnostics.

TIME SYNC

Three days. He had lost three days. He was in his apartment, standing on his charging pad. Early morning light was coming in through the window. There were voices. One high-pitched, almost like bird song. The other not quite as high, but more familiar. As his linguistic systems came online, he understood the voices.

"I think he's waking up!" There was a squeal and rapid movement.

GR-ND finished his startup and Pops saw Daphne come to a skidding halt in front of him. Her face was so clean her skin nearly glowed, and her hair was brushed and hung loose. Even her coveralls were cleaned.

Someone else stopped behind Daphne, lightly touching the girl's shoulders with light blue robotic hands. Much more refined than his old worn-out digits.

Pops took in the rest of the figure. Much newer model, elegant even, in the design. Feminine, but it didn't mimic humans. It looked like what it was, an embodied mentic.

"Mary?"

"GR-MA, if you want to get technical," she said. "I told Daphne and the other kids to call me Grama. That's okay, don't you think?"

Daphne smiled up at them both, looking from Mary to him. "Grama got you a tune up!"

Pops ran a quick system check. Most of the amber warnings were gone. Those left were a soft—less threatening—yellow. He lifted one foot from the ground, bending his knee, then repeated it with the other. Both moved smoothly.

"You haven't been taking care of yourself," Mary chided. "That's got to change. We need to be at our best to help these kids. Right, Daphne?"

"Right!" Daphne reached up and took his hand, then Mary's.

Mary couldn't smile, but she didn't need to as she reached out for his hand. He felt her smile like the memory of a scent.

....

About the Author

Ryan M. Williams is a full-time career librarian and a multi-genre writer with over twenty books. He writes across a range of genres including science fiction, fantasy, paranormal, mystery, horror, and romance. He earned a Master of Arts degree in writing popular fiction from Seton Hill University and a Master of Library and Information Science from San Jose University. His short fiction has appeared in Pulphouse Fiction Magazine, On Spec Magazine, and anthologies from Pocket Books and WMG Publishing.

Return to the Table of Contents

Also by Ryan M. Williams

POEVILLE

The POEVILLE series with feline detective C. Auguste Dupin and his human librarian Penny Copper might be just the thing.

- The Murders in the Reed Moore Library
- The Task of Auntie Dido

MOREAU SOCIETY

Brock Marsden, a genetically-modified detective, solves the toughest cases in a this far future space opera series.

- Dark Matters
- The Gingerbread House
- Past Lives
- Past Dark

DEAD THINGS

Do you like your fantasy dark and paranormal? Ravyn Washington isn't like other students. Her grandmother was called a witch and if the Inquisition discovers Ravyn's abilities she could burn in the DEAD THINGS series.

- Waking Dead Things
- Dreaming Dead Things
- Killing Dead Things

FILMING DEAD THINGS

Filming the Inquisition at work made Stefan Roland's ground-breaking documentary directing career—calling him the Jane Goodall of Dead Things.

- Farm of the Dead Things
- Mall of the Dead Things
- War of the Dead Things
- Trailer Park of the Dead Things

SCIENCE FICTION STORIES & NOVELS

Discover more science fiction with these books.

- Infestation
- Europan Holiday
- Stowaway to Eternity
- Crunch Bang: The Chrystal Eagle Stories
- Space Monkeys: A Short Science Fiction First Contact Story

• Invasion of the Book Snatchers: A Short Science Fiction Story of Small-Town Terror

ROMANCE BY KATE N. RYAN

And if you like romance and comedy, the books by KATE N. RYAN will tickle your funny bone—and more.

• Watching You Sleep: a laugh out loud romantic comedy

• Tom Scratch: A Short Fantastic Romance Story